We Look After Property
...We Don't Damage Things

By Donna Luck
With illustrations by Juliet Doyle

THE GOLDEN GR RULES SERIES

Mona Monkey and Louis Lion were having a lovely time at the making table.

They were busy with glue and scissors and all kinds of different paper and string.

They were joining pieces of paper together and there was sticky tape and glitter everywhere.

All of a sudden, Miss Beanie said, "Tidy-up time everyone!"

Everyone rushed to put things back in their proper places.

Mona Monkey and Louis Lion looked at the mess they had made.

They bundled it all up, wrapped it in the newspaper that was on the table and threw the whole lot in the bin!

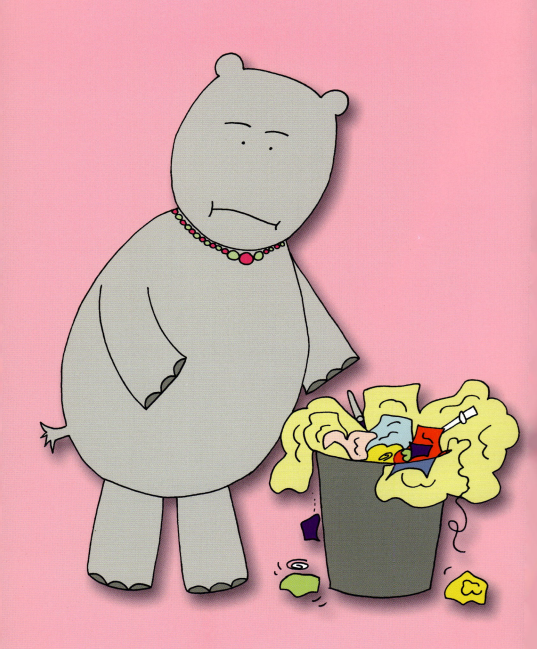

At the end of the day, Miss Beanie noticed that the bin was overflowing.

She tried to push the rubbish in a bit more.

As she did so, she noticed that there were scissors and glue sticks and paperclips and nice pieces of shiny paper all wrapped up in newspaper.

Miss Beanie frowned and thought about what she had found.

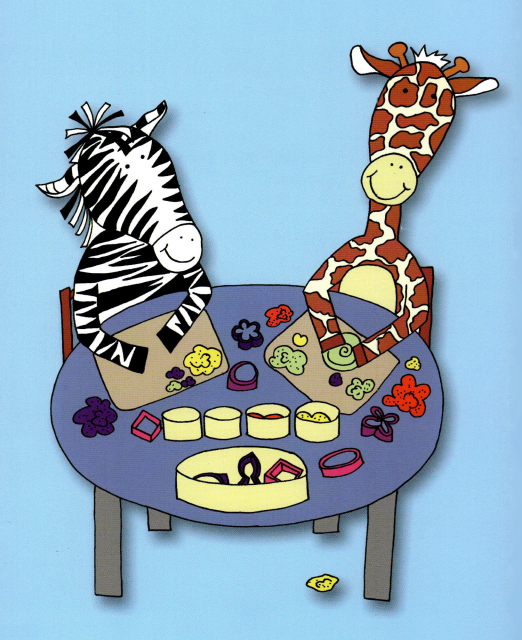

The next day, Gino Giraffe and Zelda Zebra were having a fantastic time with the play dough.

It was glittery play dough in a whole rainbow of colours.

There were great cutters in all different shapes too.

Gino and Zelda were using the cutters and some tools to make snails and snakes and people with long hair.

Then they heard Miss Beanie call, "Tidy-up time everyone, it's playtime now."

Just as before, the animals quickly collected the toys and games together.

They put them into their pots and boxes and returned them to the shelves and cupboards.

But Gino and Zelda were so busy playing that they had run out of time to tidy away.

They pushed and squished and squeezed the play dough together.

All the different colours got squashed together and then crammed into the pots.

Then, Gino and Zelda threw the cutters into the box without scraping off the bits of dough.

The next morning, Miss Beanie started to get the play dough table ready.

She was shocked to see that all the different colours were mixed-up.

She frowned.

She frowned again.

And she looked very thoughtful.

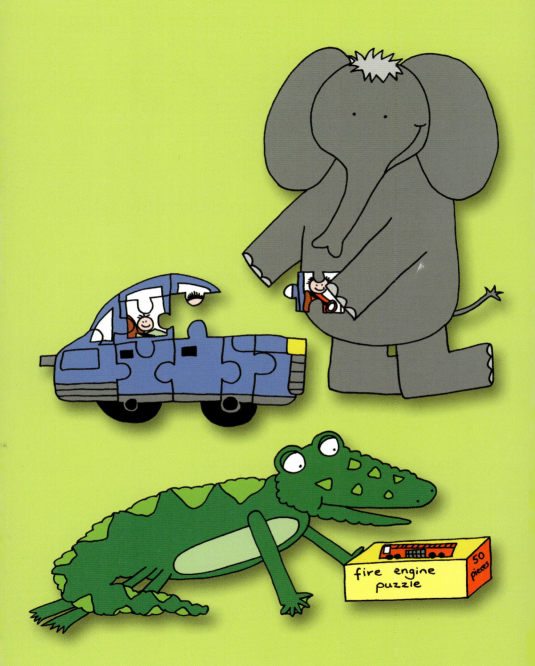

Later on that day, Alfred Alligator and Elsa Elephant were having a wonderful time on the carpet playing with the jigsaw puzzle in the shape of a car.

They loved trying to piece it together.

When they had finished it, they pulled the fire engine puzzle off the shelf and lay on the floor to do it.

It took a while to do. There were lots of pieces.

When they had finished it, Alfred and Elsa pulled two more puzzles off the shelf and began fitting all the pieces together.

They were really enjoying themselves.

Then they heard Miss Beanie say, "Tidy-up time everyone, it's snack time now."

Once again, the animals tidied away the toys and returned things to their shelves.

Alfred and Elsa looked at all the jigsaw pieces lying on the floor.

They were all mixed-up.

Oh no!

They quickly gathered the bits together.

They put the puzzle pieces back into the boxes without checking whether they belonged together.

Then they put the boxes back on the shelves.

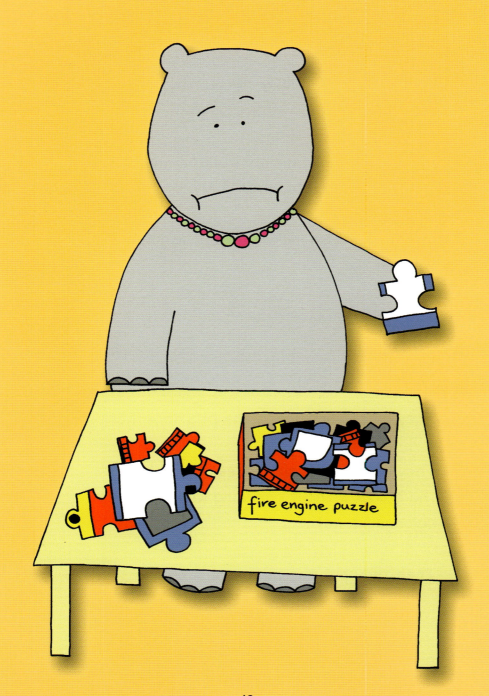

The next day, Miss Beanie took the fire engine puzzle from the shelf.

She put it on the table for the animals to do later.

She found that there were big pieces and small pieces of puzzle all mixed together.

Lots of the fire engine pieces were missing too.

Once again, Miss Beanie looked thoughtful.

Then she looked a bit cross.

Then she nodded to herself as she thought of a good idea.

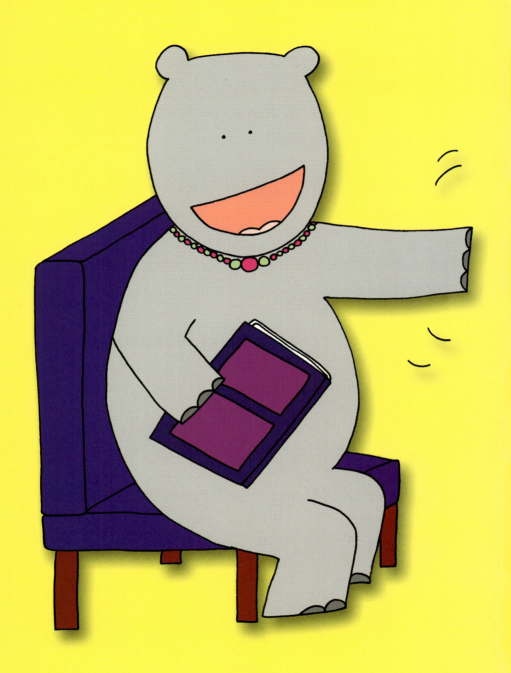

All of the animals were sitting on the carpet.

They were listening to Miss Beanie who was reading a story.

They were really looking forward to the activities they would be doing that day.

Miss Beanie finished the story.

"OK! Off you go and play! Choose carefully," she said.

The animals jumped up.

They looked around the classroom at the activities they could choose.

Elsa Elephant and Louis Lion walked around and looked on the tables.

There was nothing there!

Alfred Alligator and Gino Giraffe went over to the making table.

It was bare!

And Zelda Zebra and Mona Monkey ran over to the carpet to do some puzzles.

But the carpet was empty!

The animals all looked very puzzled.

The animals all crowded around Miss Beanie.

"There aren't any activities!" said Louis Lion.

"What can we play with?" asked Mona Monkey.

"Where is everything?" wondered Zelda Zebra.

Miss Beanie asked the animals to sit down and she explained what she had seen.

Can you remember?

She told them she had found scissors, shiny paper and glue sticks in the bin.

She showed them the mixed-up play dough.

Then she showed them the muddled puzzles.

She said that she felt very sad.

"If you don't take care of the classroom's property then there will be nothing left to play with," said Miss Beanie.

The animals were shocked!

Some looked embarrassed.

"I didn't mix up the play dough," shouted Mona Monkey.

"I didn't muddle the puzzles," called Gino Giraffe.

"We all need to keep the Golden Rule about looking after property," said Miss Beanie. "If we all help and remind each other then it will be easier."

The animals agreed.

They didn't want to be in a classroom where there were no toys to play with or wonderful activities to do.

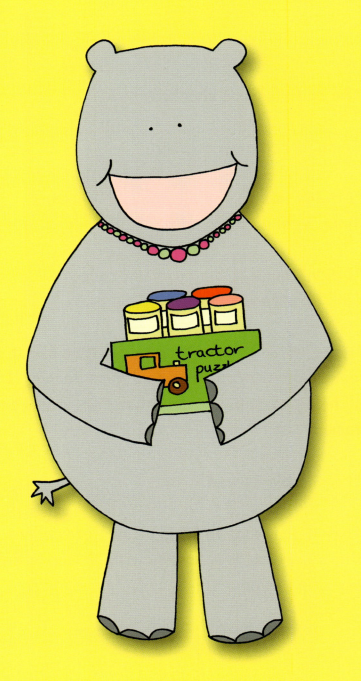

All week the animals worked together, helping each other to look after their property.

Miss Beanie watched them and noticed how much better they were behaving.

After making them play with the mixed-up play dough for a week, she rewarded them with some new rainbow-coloured play dough and a super new puzzle in the shape of a tractor.

And do you know? Weeks later, the play dough and the puzzle still look brand new!